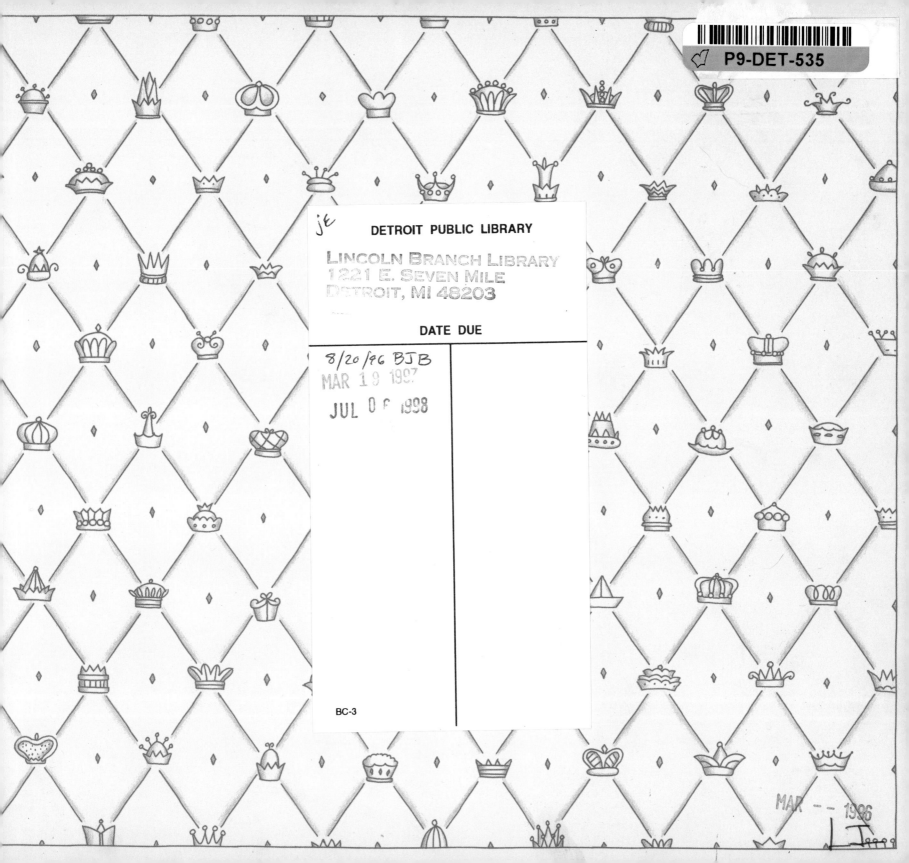

THE EMPEROR PENGUIN'S
NEW CLOTHES

jε

VIKING
Published by the Penguin Group
Penguin Books USA Inc., 375 Hudson Street, New York, New York 10014, U.S.A.
Penguin Books Ltd, 27 Wrights Lane, London W8 5TZ, England
Penguin Books Australia Ltd, Ringwood, Victoria, Australia
Penguin Books Canada Ltd, 10 Alcorn Avenue, Toronto, Ontario, Canada M4V 3B2
Penguin Books (N.Z.) Ltd, 182-190 Wairau Road, Auckland 10, New Zealand

Penguin Books Ltd, Registered Offices: Harmondsworth, Middlesex, England

First published in Canada by Kids Can Press Ltd., 1994
First published in the United States of America by Viking,
a division of Penguin Books USA Inc., 1995

1   3   5   7   9   10   8   6   4   2

The illustrations in this book were drawn on matte acetate
with ink and colored pencils and were back-painted with acrylic paints.

Copyright © Janet Perlman, 1994
All rights reserved
Library of Congress Catalog Card Number: 94-60400

ISBN 0-670-85864-1
Printed in Hong Kong

THE EMPEROR PENGUIN'S
NEW CLOTHES

RETOLD AND ILLUSTRATED BY

JANET PERLMAN

VIKING

THERE WAS ONCE an Emperor Penguin who was so fond of fine clothes that he spent nearly all his money on them. He had a different outfit for every hour of the day, and if he didn't have anything new to wear, he was soon filled with boredom.

"It is the clothes that make the penguin!" he would often say.

He had no time for his soldiers or his royal subjects. If anyone asked where the Emperor was, the answer was nearly always, "He is in his dressing room."

One day two scoundrels came to town. They announced that they were master weavers who could make a special magic cloth—not only was it unusually beautiful, but it was completely invisible to those who were either dishonest or simpleminded. Now that was a rare thing indeed!

All the penguins were very impressed, although none could afford the high prices the weavers were asking.

When news of the magic cloth reached the Emperor Penguin, he thought, "That is the thing for me! With a suit made of this cloth, I will be able to tell who in my court can be trusted, and who are the foolish ones. I must order some of this cloth at once!"

So the Emperor commanded the weavers to make some of their special cloth for him. Large amounts of gold were paid to them, and they were given the finest silk thread with which to weave the cloth.

The scoundrels set up two huge weaving looms, but they kept the silk for themselves. They sat at the looms day and night, pretending to be very busy, though there was no thread on the machines at all.

After a time, the Emperor wondered how his cloth was coming along, so he sent three trusted High Officials to inspect it for him.

The weavers greeted them with much excitement.

"See for yourselves," they exclaimed. "The Emperor's cloth is the most beautiful we have ever woven."

But when the High Officials looked at the looms, their beaks dropped. They could see nothing—nothing at all! The weavers pointed out fine details: the pattern here, the colors there.

The High Officials put on their spectacles, but they could not see a single thread.

"Is it possible that I am dishonest or a simpleton?" each one thought to himself. "Perhaps I am not fit to be a High Official! The Emperor must never find out!"

So one of them said, "Marvelous! Such . . . brilliant colors!"
And the others quickly added, "Yes, simply . . . simply . . .
exquisite! Glorious! We will tell the Emperor how wonderful
his cloth will be!"

The Emperor was delighted to hear the good news and sent the weavers more gold and silk to finish their work. Again, they kept the silk for themselves and did no weaving at all.

Time passed, and the Emperor grew impatient to see his cloth, so he decided to visit the weavers himself. He took with him his wisest advisers, including the three High Officials who had been there before.

When the Emperor arrived at the shop, the weavers
bowed low and invited everyone to inspect the looms.
"Isn't this the most magnificent cloth you have ever
seen?" they said proudly.

"Oh yes!" exclaimed the High Officials. And one added, "Why, the colors are even more vivid than I remembered!"

Everyone else was speechless. They looked at the looms from every side, and underneath as well, but no one could see even the tiniest bit of cloth. The Emperor rubbed his eyes in disbelief.

"Good heavens!" he thought. "If the others can see the cloth, why can't I? Am I dishonest? Or simpleminded? This is terrible! No one must find out!"

So he said, "Why, the cloth is splendid! What fine
workmanship! Superb!"

And the others added their praise. "Indeed! How striking
the pattern is! Delightful!"

The Emperor immediately ordered that a suit and a long
trailing cape be made from the cloth.

"I will wear my new clothes in a Grand Parade for all
to see!" he exclaimed.

"A brilliant idea!" said the weavers, and they measured
him for the suit right then and there.

Soon every penguin in the land was talking about the
Grand Parade.

In the days that followed, the weavers could be seen busily cutting the air with their scissors, stitching with empty needles, and pretending to sew on buttons and trim. The night before the parade, they burned extra candles so passersby would be sure to see how hard they were working.

In the morning the weavers hurried to the palace and
announced, "The Emperor's new clothes are ready."

"See, here is the jacket," said one, pretending to hold up
the garment.

"And here is the cape," said the other.

"Oh dear, I cannot see the clothes," thought the Emperor. "But everyone else can, so they must be there."

The weavers helped him into the suit, piece by piece.

"A perfect fit!" said one.

"A most flattering color!" said the other.

"Indeed," said the Emperor. "These clothes are as light as a feather. Brrr! Is there a draft in here?"

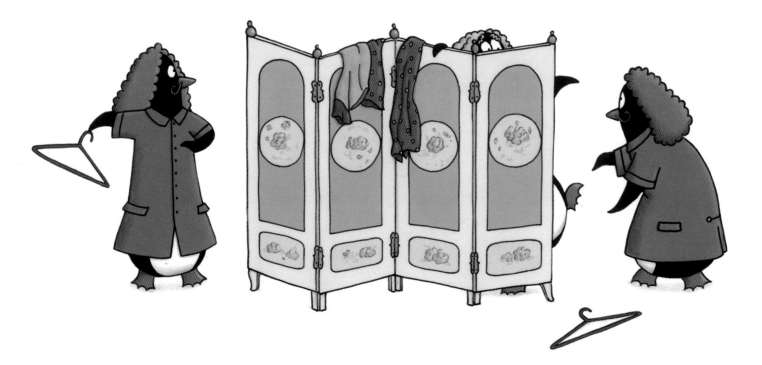

The Penguins of the Court were full of praise for the
Emperor's new clothes.

"The very height of fashion!" they raved. "Sensational!
Sheer perfection!"

Trumpets sounded, and the Grand Parade was underway. Everywhere, penguins crowded the streets, waiting to see the Emperor's new clothes. What a magnificent, stately procession it was! First came soldiers and marching bands in splendid uniforms, followed by dancers and acrobats in colorful costumes.

Then came the Official Penguins of the Court in long
flowing robes, and, at last, the Emperor. He walked proudly,
his beak held high, his royal trainbearers pretending to carry
the long cape. A hush fell over the crowd as he approached.

Everyone stared in amazement. No one could see the
Emperor's clothes at all. But then a few penguins started to
cheer, and others joined in. No one wanted to be thought
dishonest or simpleminded.

"Look at the Emperor's new clothes! How majestic he is!"
came the cries of admiration from every side. Everybody
waved at the Emperor, and the Emperor waved back.

Suddenly a small voice rose from the crowd.
"But look, the Emperor isn't wearing any clothes!"
The voice came from a very young penguin.

Some of the crowd stopped cheering as the penguin called out louder, "Can't you see? The Emperor isn't wearing any clothes at all!"

Now the Emperor heard him too. He was shocked to hear such a thing. But soon others were repeating what the young penguin had said, first in whispers, and then louder, until the whole crowd was shouting, "He's right, the Emperor has no clothes!"

The Emperor's beak turned bright red, for he knew it must be true.

Now he could only march proudly on, his royal trainbearers behind him carrying nothing at all. As for the scoundrels, they were never seen in the town again.

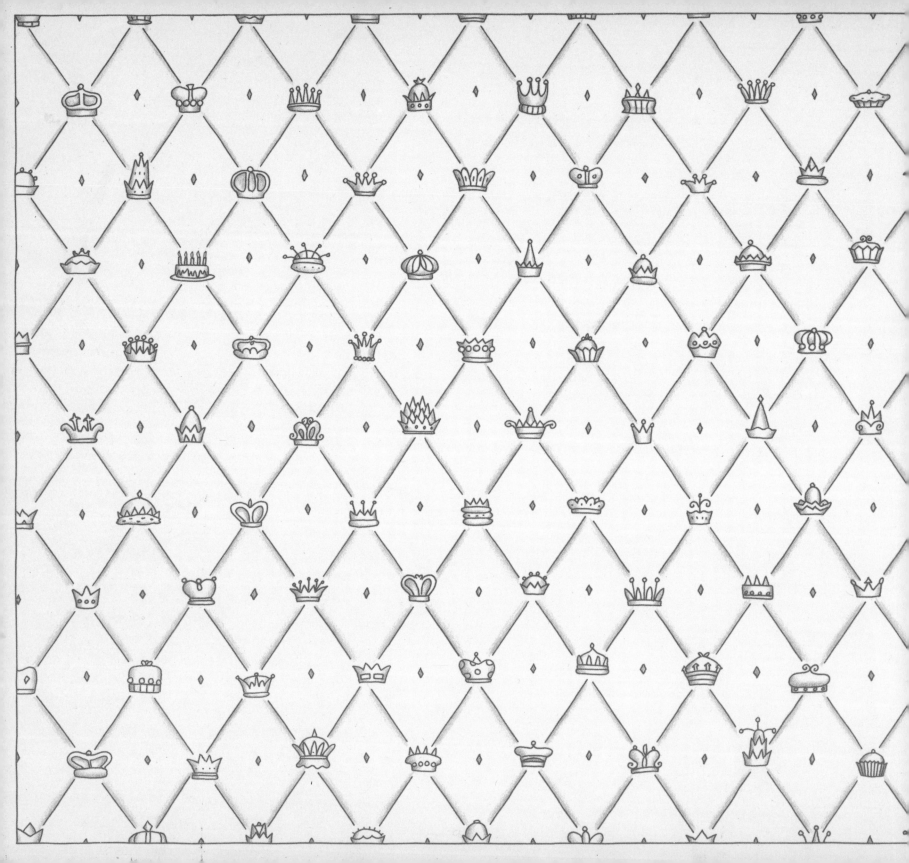